Poetic Inju:
New and Origir

Author : Sandy Jonss<

CW00863898

Scarlett Ribbons Publications

Copyright© Sandy Jonsson 2022

"A publisher would rather see a burglar in his office than a poet" Don Marquis

Here is a book to kill time, for those who like it better dead.

I hope you enjoy my observations…

"The comeback should always be stronger than the setback, make it so" Sandy x

THE DAISY CHAIN

If hearts had stems as daisies do

To link us up and see us through

We'd all join up and make a chain

And life would be all right again

Dedications:

In loving memory of Scarlett JP and Erik Georg Jönsson.

Fondest remembrance: Alan Hearn, Rhys Pollard, Robbie-Jay and Becky.

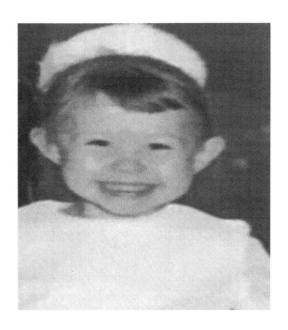

Aged three, reciting my first poem at a wedding. So began a
lifelong love of rhyming. Poetry generally gets a raw deal.
Let's shake it up and see how it goes…what could possibly
go wrong?

TITANIUM GIRL

You dazzle us with magic light, your courage is a beacon

Your laughter is a special gift, you shine in every season

For you are made of steel and stone, and you are standing tall

While life has thrown some rocks at you, you smile despite it all

Your love's eternal, strong and true, though life has been unkind

You're diamond bright, titanium, your dazzle leaves us blind.

And all the love you hold inside is clear for us to see

The sparkle in your eyes confirms the best is yet to be

BROKEN

I always thought there'd still be time, to see a happy ending

That one day you would find your smile and feel the love we're sending.

But now I know your ship has sailed to destination : broken

The tracks are gone, the train de-railed, and so much left unspoken

Cruel fate has been a fickle friend who stole the sun within

And life has been so brutal, time is such a cruel villain

A memory is a moment saved in souls that can't forget

As love lives on despite it all, the best and brightest yet

You're deeply etched upon our souls and we cannot forget you

We crave your counsel like a drug and want to come and get you

But we are just so helpless here, so small and so unable

Not worthy now to gather up the crumbs beneath your table

And in our hearts you shall remain, a shining light to guide us

The courage in your silent eyes, a burning flame inside us

Please be at peace, and rest assured your heart stays in our heart

We'll carry forward all you taught, absent, but not apart

We know the world has lost it's shine, all meaning rendered senseless

Our journey's made on bitter ground, no open space, just fences

Remembering the brighter days, the warm sun and the laughter

We saw the light side of the moon, the happy ever after

Our gratitude remains with us when all our tears are dry

We know you couldn't stay with us, but your memory shall not die

FAMILY

"Sometimes it is the shelter to the storm, but sometimes it *is* the storm itself" Thomas Shelby ~ Peaky Blinders

MY FRIEND

My friend you may be far away, as far as you can be

So far away that we can't even share a pot of tea

That does not mean I could forget the memories we have shared

It can't diminish what we had, or all the times you cared

We met one day, so long ago, and ended up true friends

We found a strong connection, it's the kind that never ends

Remember all those hours you spent just wishing time away?

Forget them now, for they are gone, and these words come to say:

The hopes and dreams I have for you have always been the best

And now your wishes have come true, your future will be blessed

I'll miss our moments in the sun, the laughs and chats we had

The way we always shared our news, the good times and the bad

But life's a challenge you must face, this life can be so testing

I'm mindful of the sacrifice, and how much you're investing

A brave, new world is calling you to pastures warm and sunny

To have a glorious future in the land of milk and honey

But if you ever miss this place and wonder how we are

Just take a look into the sky and find the brightest star

I'll look up at the morning sun and know you're looking too

And all those miles will melt away, and I'll be there with you.

STOLEN TREASURE

Heaven sent, then heaven stole a precious Dad from you

For he was needed up above, because his heart was true

But he is never far from home, he watches you with pride

He knows how hard you had to try to keep your tears inside

So when the days seem hard to bear and all the roads are long

Remember how he loved you so, and that your soul is strong

Smile for all those special days, that shone without an end

They serve to bring the strength you need to be your own
best friend

The future lies ahead of you - you've still so far to go

Be guided by his golden heart , the Dad who loved you so.

MY BABY STAR

Once there was a tiny star who would not go to sleep

He couldn't seem to close his eyes, and always tried to peep

It can't be time for bed just yet, is what he always said

The night is still so young and I *don't* want to go to bed

But little star, you need your sleep, it's time you got some rest

Or how will you be shiny bright so you can look your best?

Those magic beams that keep you strong must be allowed to grow

Or soon you'll see, before too long, you will no longer glow

Remember it's your special job to always twinkle brightly

So go to sleep my little one, it's what you should do nightly.

LOVED YOU BEFORE I MET YOU

If you knew how long I waited for your smile to touch the earth

You would know you were created to bring wonder with your birth

Though I rarely get to tell you : you're the moon, the stars, the sun

You should know you fill my world with love and laughter, joy and fun

So if I forget to thank you, it's a fault you must forgive

Sometimes, I'm so busy living that I just forget to live

You are precious, more than diamonds, you who healed my broken soul

You have shown me just what matters, you have made my small heart whole

I'm so thankful every second, that I get to see you grow

My heart's full of love that's bursting, so much love, you'll never know.

GIVE THE CHILDREN LOVE, MORE LOVE AND STILL
MORE LOVE, AND THE COMMON SENSE WILL
COME BY ITSELF

PIPPI LONGSTOCKING ~ ASTRID LINDGREN

MAGICIAN

You are such a special genius, and the finest in the land

You don't simply have a hairbrush, you hold a magic wand

You sort the crazy hairstyles, limpest curls and lifeless locks

Make magic out of nothing, what you do just simply rocks

You take those dodgy barnets : turn them into princess tresses

You make an awesome up-do from the sorry bird nest messes

So thank you for the special flourish you bring to our lives

Without your magic talents we could clearly not survive.

BLUEBELL

At the end of the lane, behind the trees, where the bluebells grow really high

There's a tiny place you would not spot if you were just passing by

There lives a fairy in those woods and her name is Minxy-Belle

She's smart and cute and VERY wise, with lots of tales to tell

She hugs her friends as they have tea just along the secret path

She is the dearest little soul with a super- tinkly laugh

Her dress is made of rainbow silk with matching silken slippers

Her floaty wings just catch the light : the grass looks like it glitters

So when the sky is clear and blue or if you see a rainbow

Perhaps you'll spot her with her friends as they play there in the hollow.

FLAMINGO AMIGO

Life can be so boring if you are like the rest

So be a pink flamingo and you will be the best

Flamingos are amazing, they stand out in the crowd

They brighten up your spirit and make your heart feel proud

So next time you are out there, fluff up your finest feathers

Life is really just fantastic when flamingos flock together.

M-AZING

Life can sometimes bring an angel to the earth in human
form

I've been blessed to be so lucky with a friend so kind and
warm

You have brought a magic sparkle to my life, you changed
my world

All the good advice you gave me, you're a clever, funny girl

I can never thank you fully for the way you saved the day

With your wisdom and your kindness, lessons learned the
lasting way

In my memory there's a picture, two blonde soulmates, you
and I

Times have changed, but you're eternal, you shine like a
diamond sky.

A POSTCARD FROM HOME (for Mr M)

There's a perfect sense of peace this time you gaze on the horizon

A hopeful glow to contrast with the weight of pain you're hiding

Time can't erase the memories so engraved upon your heart

For all the sacrifice you made to give your boys a start

No mention ever made of all the suffering you went through

But life has brought the best to them and it's all thanks to you

Their gratitude shines from their eyes for all who care to see

But dark souls hold such secrets knowing tiny boys are free

There's painful recollection of those brutal times gone by

The bitterness of sorrow, being forced to say goodbye

But courage and commitment helped to save the ones you love

With arms of strength, and blessings being sent from up above

Such a dear, courageous father, with a heart so strong and true

The generations yet to come will owe so much to you

So we must make a promise now, ensure the moments matter

A solid vow to still hold firm when all our feelings shatter

A bitter price, such sacrifice - can simply not be measured

When all your love is gathered in, the gift forever treasured

It seems there is no justice in this crazy world of ours

As heaven's hand reached out to write your name up in the stars.

While gazing on the water, we will find a peaceful thought

And cherish all the love we shared and courage that you taught.

ELEPHANT IN THE ROOM

Hello to the ELEPHANT IN THE ROOM, I finally got to meet you

I hear you don't get out so much that's why I'm here to greet you

You've had a really lonely time, we all tried to ignore you

But now I think you'll be just fine, and I hope we don't bore you

For we are pretty self-obsessed and full of our own issues

In fact you could say we're depressed, all crying in our tissues

We could try recognising you and giving you a mention

It's not like we're providing you with our love or attention

We knew that you were standing there, so still behind the curtain

Your feet, we noticed, to be fair, but we were just uncertain

We were unsure that we could stop this strategy we started

And yet we let your name drop, it must leave you broken-
hearted

But now we've met you face to face I see we shouldn't hate
you

We know you're always in this place, so we can reinstate you

We'd learn a lot if we'd accept that we just need to try

Mr Elephant I will shake your hand the next time I pass by.

HELLO R-J

Hello son, I see you now just rapping on the path

Headphones firmly on your head, and that amazing laugh

Here you are just rushing past, you hug me as you go

With such a bond just built to last, no one could ever know

Bright and funny, pure of spirit, and eternal joy to me

Heart so big and sunny, you were all I dreamed you'd be

Making my life sweet and bringing sunshine on your way

I watched you as you found your feet, grew prouder every day

Little notes you used to write, to tell us you were near

We cherish since you went away, your clothes are all still here

For you have left us far too soon, still had so much to do

I'm thankful to the universe that I was mum to you

So hard to live without you, but I know your soul is free

You're in my heart forever – little boy, you'll always be

MAN-CHILD

Gazing at the stars tonight, they shine like they're brand new

To celebrate the special joy that we all found in you

Eternal child with eyes so bright, a heart so soft and caring

A lovely smile that hid the weight of pain that you were
bearing

This world for you was changing and somehow you let us
know

That though you loved us dearly it was time for you to go

And when the new tomorrow starts without you by our side

We'll know you're standing near us and your love will be a
guide

Your favourite things will carry on reminding us of days

When life was so much easier in oh so many ways

In building bricks you built a world made up of childhood
dreams

That little boy inside of you was closer than he seems

The signs of you remain with us long after time has ended

And broken hearts we feel today will one day soon be mended

We won't forget to think of you on all your special days

The crazy, fun and happy times, before the misty haze

The gentle sun will bring you back for just a little while

We'll raise a glass to heaven, and we'll think of you.......

And smile.

FEELING GREY

A tiny cloud of grey appeared and stopped above my head

It floated there for several days and then moved on ahead

It crossed the sky in front of me and it blocked out the sun

I could not say for certain why it covered everyone

The cloud moved with me as I walked, it went with me to school

It followed me throughout the day and made me feel a fool

I wandered on my own a while and tried to get away

That cloud just covered up my smile, and lasted all the day

The other people looked the same, confused about the sky

And I thought it was such a shame that no one wondered why

Then suddenly between the clouds a little shard of light

With piercing raindrops scattered, in the rainbow, shining bright

The cloud that had been following was nowhere to be seen

The sun once more began to shine, my fears were just a dream.

………..

NAN MOVES

Have you ever pulled a Nan move just like your sweet old dear?

And got yourself in Nan groove so that you can feel her near

Have you ever licked a tissue, to wipe away a smudge or two?

Maybe hygiene is an issue, but it's what your Nan would do

Did you ever stand there waving, 'til your children left the street

Like a crazy Mexican Stand-Off, that's really rather sweet?

Do you have a bag of toffees carried with you "just in case"?

Or a tiny little hanky with a corner made of lace?

Do you sigh about the weather 'cos the damp gets in your bones?

And complain at kids forever 'cos they're always on their phones

Did you sit there watching Bake Off, admiring all those pastry skills?

And then moaned and turned the lights off, trying to save on pesky bills

Did you ever spy a robin out there on the garden tree?

And then started gently sobbing 'cos your Nan has been set free?

Remembering all those special things your sweet Nan used to do

Will remind you in a funny way that your Nan's still with you.

WALKING WITH MY NONNA

I like walking with my Nonna

Her steps are short like mine

She does not try to hurry me

She simply takes her time

How I love to walk with Nonna

She sees the way I do

A tiny bird, a pretty flower

Each sparkling drop of dew

Some people only hurry

There is much they don't see

I'm so glad God made my Nonna….

So unrushed and young like me.

TEA WITH THE QUEEN

Let's take a little moment

We'll stop to have some tea

And a giant marmalade sandwich

Big enough for you and me.

I will pour the teapot carefully

With my paws, I'll take good care

I am awfully glad you found the time

When you'd barely time to spare!

We could make an extra sandwich

So that you can take it home

I am sure you'd like some marmalade

When you're sitting on the throne.

BEACH LIFE

I think I'll be a mermaid and frolic in the sea

I will comb my hair and flick my tail for everyone to see

I'll splash in shining water and jump around in pools

Maybe captivate some sailors and then chase the dolphin schools

My tail will be so lovely, several shades of green and blue

And I'll while away the hours finding happy things to do

The summer sun can be so pretty, dancing on the wave

But there's no-one to talk to and its friendship that I crave

So I'll feel pretty lonely as I'm living out my dream

And I'll never find a husband because mermaids can't be seen

So there'll be no mermaid babies, that's another broken wish

Sadly no-one wants a cuddle when you always smell of fish

So I guess I'll just be me then, keep my feet on solid ground

But once a year I'll "mermaid" when vacations come around.

LAND-LOCKED

The sea calls out to the sailor's soul as the ocean whispers his name

And a silent bell rings a silent toll to the heart it can never tame

The moon's wild light sheds ghostly beams as the rocks take their cruellest form

To crush the sailor and all his dreams, through the calm that belies the storm

His crystal eyes look deep within, for his wise precious heart is true

As a thousand memories gather in to reflect in his eyes of blue

Abandoning hope when land is nigh, with his spirit drained of light

While his heavy heart, with a broken sigh, must surrender all its fight

Still a distant shore will call him on through the untamed waves of foam

And the restless hunger lingers long as his siren calls him home

LEGACY

Money's not free, but love costs so much more

My heart does not care if I'm rich or I'm poor

As I look in your eyes and I still see the shore:

I wish I could leave something behind

It's such a brave concept that man can belong

If I had any answers, I'd write you a song

For my heart is the best, and you knew all along:

I would try to leave something behind

Don't try to tell me that I have been blind

They say there's a soulmate that I'll someday find

But if I search forever I'll just lose my mind:

Still I strive to leave something behind

Time is so lost with the rules we invent

Words hold the answers to all my intent

When my son is a man he will know what I meant:

When I tried to leave something behind

THE AFTER PARTY

I hope there's red carpet in heaven

And they roll it out when you arrive

That they serve fancy cocktails and drinks
there

Just to celebrate that you were alive

I hope every companion you made here

Who decided to go on ahead

Is now waiting for you at a party

And all dressed up in their finest thread

I hope all your fond memories are with you

To remind you of all you have done

That there's laughter and joy every moment

And the sky's always filled up with sun

I hope the music they're playing is jolly

And the snacks are all served on a tray

That the glasses are made of fine crystal

You should know you deserve them that way

Take your time there to drink in the moment

Let the crowd share your witty remark

Dance your heart out and sparkle so brightly

But don't linger too long in the dark

For if they have a window to show you

How we're missing you here all day long

Please don't look through that window too closely

For its inside our hearts you belong

Such a sparkle you brought to our lifetime

Filling our days with laughter and mirth

Share your humour with angels in heaven

Make them smile as you did here on earth

Pour those drinks and keep dancing my
dearest

Laughing with your new friends in the sky

How we wished you could always be near us

But there was simply no time for goodbye.

SADNESS

Oh the days seem so long here without you

And the nights are much colder somehow

Every thought that we have is about you

And our hearts are so broken, just now

It's a shock that you left us so quickly

Lost and lonely we're likely to stay

Our goodbyes are just drops in the ocean

Filled with words we're not ready to say

We will try to be stronger and thankful

For the joys that you brought to our lives

But we can't see that now, it's too early

Such a pain we can't even describe

We miss every wise word that you gave us

And the warmth of your kind, caring voice

All that light in your smile that brought comfort

When the world seemed to give us no choice

There's a hole that can never be filled now

Such a space in our lives where you were

We just miss how you made things seem better

When we thought you would always be there

You should know we are missing you madly

For the gap that you left is too great

But we know you will greet us all gladly

When it's our turn, we know you will wait

But for now there is no consolation

We cannot see the way through the cloud

Seems the only way we can be near you

Is by saying your dear name out loud

They say time will heal us just a little

And we won't always feel this raw sorrow

For you taught us to look out for rainbows

And to hope for a brighter tomorrow

Still these days seem so long here without you

And the nights always bring such a chill

There can be no more doubt that we loved you

And no question that we always will.

LOST IN SPACE

I'm sitting in my comfy chair

As calm as I can be

I'm drifting off in sleepy bliss

You're sitting next to me

A soft breeze blows across my cheek

As I sit on the porch

The fireflies light up the sky

Each one a gleaming torch

A strange glow shimmers in the air

As I look to the stars

I wonder just how far we are

From Jupiter and Mars

The morning sun approaches

But the night's not over yet

We're smiling at each other

It's a look I can't forget

We stay here 'til the daylight hour

The wine is sweet tonight

My head is in a spin

And yet my eyes are clear and bright

I feel you sitting next to me

And I am lost in space

The dark curl of your eyelash

And the soft curve of your face

We're singing now and laughing

At the victories of our day

But you cannot stay long this time

You have to go away

I feel your hand reach out to mine

The moonlight frames your hair

And softly through a sparkling strand

The static fills the air

I strain my eyes to look again

I'm overwhelmed by fear

It comes to me as clear as day

That you're not really here

The memory of all we shared

Has played a trick on me

I know you love me dearly

But this was not meant to be

I shake my head and go inside

My cosy bed is calling

The weight of sleep takes over me

And I am softly falling

Sweet peace of mind will not be mine

Perhaps in time I'll learn

So I try to fall asleep again

And pray you will return...

A GREEN TOWER

If someone had thought for a minute

To put stained glass windows inside

The poor people there, living in it

Would probably never have died

The pain and the shame keeps increasing

Corporations are guilty, no doubt

Brave fireman were blamed for retreating

But that's not what this scandal's about

Like pawns to be left and discarded

In a ruthless and cruel game of chess

A human life is disregarded

When you're poor you are simply "worth less".

UNBEARABLE LIGHTNESS OF BEING

Here's a truth to take on board

It will not bring good cheer

For life can be a two-edged sword

With blonde locks at your ear

For never will a grown-up boy

Give more than passing care

Or love you for your heart and mind

When you have golden hair!

ORCHID CHILD

You're like a rare orchid that grows

Such a challenge that nobody knows

Because you're on the spectrum

You have a collection

Of rules keeping me on my toes

Just today, I can't take it for now

There's a permanent crease in my brow

But I paint on my best face

Knowing I am your safe place

We will find a way through this somehow

That behaviour is driving me barmy

So maybe I should call out the army

Is this some kind of test

Lord I'm doing my best

Then you give me "that look" and disarm me

I sit here with my head in my hands

Like every broken SEN mum in the land

Love life up on the blocks

While I'm ironing your socks

Gee, this isn't the future I planned!

My social life's gone very quiet

And I live on a very strange diet

Of pink wine and coffee

And date expired toffee

Those who think it's a "doddle" should try it

Somehow *I* am the one who's to blame

And I feel myself wrapped up in shame

I absorb all the "heat"

Learn to think on my feet

As my personal life goes down the drain

Oh those tantrums are making me ill

And today my hair doesn't look "brill"

Please, dear God, get me through this

'Cos if I don't do this

I honestly don't know who will

And no parent should beg it is true

Feels like I'm just a slave here to you

So I sit here defeated

As each scene's repeated

It is Groundhog day, what can I do?

I feel just like a downtrodden wife

Some days made out of trouble and strife

I ask "where do I start"

Yet I know in my heart

You're the best thing I have in my life

I am here doing all my research

At the end of the table I perch

As I drive myself mental

Can you reach your potential

Will the world just leave you in the lurch?

All parenting these days is tough

So hard knowing your best's not enough

But I'm happy to suffer

Yes I'll be your buffer

You are just so damn hard not to love

Those school gate mums make me ashamed

I ask why, and just what have they gained?

This system's so twisted

SEN parents : blacklisted

Seems each way that I turn, I get blamed

You are not a square peg in a hole

My life's work is protecting your soul

So I fight every battle

When they treat us like cattle

A fair future for you is my goal

Ask myself, did I do something wrong?

Was the whole thing my fault all along?

But who says this is tragic?

You're made of pure magic

And just singing your own special song

I think back to the day you were new

All the dreams in my heart held for you

There is never a time

I'm not glad you are mine

There is nothing that I will not do

Disapproval will not make us sink

Keep your chin up and give me a wink

We must shake up this whole town

Come let's go kick some doors down

And perhaps we'll teach THEM how to think!

Just one flash of that lovely big smile

I am ready to go that last mile

It's your future that matters

So who cares that I'm shattered

You are only a kid for a while

You're evolved and you're just so darn clever

I know this phase will not last forever

You did not get a choice

But for now I'm your voice

We will find a way through this together

Oh some days I have prattled and sworn

Knowing this life cannot be "the norm"

You're a pedigree being…

But that's not what they're seeing

And I still bless the day you were born.

THE BLUE PLANET

Just what have we left for our children?

Blue planet is broken and bare

Long gone are the fish from our ocean

True testament that we did not care

The wildlife are gone from our eye-line

No more are the species we knew

The birds took their song from our skyline

By thoughtless neglect through and through

We caused this by selfish consumption

The skies are now silent and grey

With ignorant hearts and assumption

We've given our future away

We ruined the planet forever

We poisoned the fish and the birds

We should be ashamed altogether

Our actions speak louder than words

Our teardrops should drown us in sorrow

To think that we did this ourselves

Just what have we left for tomorrow

Wake up. Can't you hear alarm bells ?

It's no good just sitting here mourning

The old life that we love will be lost

Take this as your own final warning

Or our kids will be counting the cost.

....

THE EAGLE SPIRIT

Please don't cry at my grave for I am not there

I'm up with the eagles, and dancing on air

I'm down with the butterflies so wild and so free

Playing tag on the wind while we're waiting for thee.

....

MISS MARILYN

Last Sunday we saw Marilyn beside the Eiffel
Tower

A lady of a certain age, who simply oozed
girl power

Her nails and hair were right on point, her
scarf flew in the air

As she made all the traffic stop, all we could
do was stare

Her style just simply caught our eye, her
elegance shone through

Designer bag and killer heels, such timeless
beauty too

I wonder where her journey led, late lunch or
lovers tryst?

And if her voice was soft and sweet, and who it was she kissed…

So was that really Marilyn?Now that would be bizarre!

To think she might walk every day, along that boulevard.

■■

RAINBOW SLIDE

Now that would be the perfect crime

I stole your heart and you stole mine

We'd hitch a ride up to the stars

And hang around some heavenly bars

Then as the morning star slides in

We'll catch a rainbow home again

And finding wordless ways to speak

We'll do it all again, next week!

■■■

Always go the extra mile… it is never
crowded…. Anon

MY SUMMER SON

Remembering those summer days that never
seemed to end

The freckled nose and golden hair of my
eternal friend

That little boy who stayed all day and played
upon the sand

So long ago and far away he held his
momma's hand

His tiny bucket treasured, building castles
meant to last

Who could have guessed those balmy days
would disappear so fast

I cherish every memory of the time he was so
small

So hard to reconcile that he could ever be so
tall

I reminisce to days gone by and then the teardrops start

I lock each moment tightly in the cradle of my heart.

. . . .

BON VOYAGE,

I hope that you will always be the captain of
your ship

No matter what life sends your way, you still
enjoy each trip

I hope you find a ray of light to guide your
sails each day

That lessons can be learned each time things
might not go your way

Be focused on the way ahead, your eyes upon
the mast

Don't let yourself be scuppered by the storms
of your own past

Voyage onwards, if the tide should turn, or
waves are rough at sea

And stay the finest version of who you were meant to be.

• •

LIMO LIFE

She's riding in a fancy car, through city lights she goes

With cocktails in the moonlight as his fascination grows

With the superficial people, brushing shoulders with the stars

Champagne fills their empty souls up, driving in their fancy cars

On a rich man's arm she sparkles like a star without a sky

Friends and family all forgotten, never stopped to say goodbye

Oh so pretty, but naïve she was…disaster just the same

For she loved him 'til he left her, victim of a rich man's game

So she ran off to the country, tried to hide the guilt and grief

There she met another rascal and this time he was a thief

Stole her heart and broke her spirit, left her wrinkled up and sad

To reflect upon her choices, never seeing they were bad.

She returned then to the city, entertaining with the best

To a fancy English mansion, filled with dull and sordid guests

In a designated building he makes laws his friends will break

As he loves her and he leaves her, still no ring, for goodness sake

So she climbs the bridge at midnight just a lost and lonely girl

Innocence is dead and buried, but her hair still holds a curl!

She is dragged out of the water, muddy slime wrenched from her lung

She survives to tell her story as the truth from her is wrung

~

In the window seat she sits there, sleepy head
bowed on her chest

Gave her best years out to scoundrels, she's
no longer getting dressed

On her finger, there's no diamond, just an
empty, wasted space

Washed up in a lonely care home, as a sad
and sorry case

But this story's not a new one, time stood still
for years and years

Rich men thrive the whole world over, sweet
girls shed a million tears

Pretty, sweet girls bare their shoulders when
the nights are deep and dark

"They only love you when you're pretty and
as cheerful as a lark"

Somewhere in the city centre there's a girl who's getting dressed

Out to meet her fancy lover - hoping he will be impressed

By the sharp cut of her outfit and the soft curl of her hair

Never knowing that's she's losing, never seeing life's unfair

But she gets into the limo parked out on the boulevard

Door is opened for her gently as the man shows her his card

She will drink the champagne slowly, she's committed to this game

So begins another cycle, a hundred years and nothing's changed

TIME TO REFLECT

The passing of time can't erase you

For your smile is engraved on my heart

And while life may have taken you from us

In the silence we are never apart

Every moment we shared is a memory

Shining golden and bright in the sky

All the pain that we feel can't be measured

Never ready to say our goodbye

We will look for your light, ever near us

As the morning sun rises each day

In the blue sky that follows the rainbow

Through the raindrops that fall in the grey

With the cold, winter wind of December

When the snow makes a blanket of white

Through those snowflakes our hearts will remember

That your courage still shone, ever bright

Such a magical presence has touched us

Bringing warmth to the time that we shared

Showing calm and composure we needed

Thoughtful guidance that proved how you cared

So today and forever our tears fall

For we miss you and we always will

We will never forget all those moments

Time for us will forever stand still.

HELLO WORLD

Put down your phones all you lads and you lasses

Give me your tired, your poor huddled masses

Bring forth the survivors who yearn to break free

Send all the hopeless and homeless to me

Find them safe refuge to rest on my shore

I have no great statue, and no golden door

Just a dry space to land near the white cliffs of Dover

But smug's the new black and humanity's over

It seems we forgot about care and compassion

Kindness is so rare now, it must be on ration

Some people have hearts that have turned into granite

As we build our empires and pillage the planet

Imagine your fear if the roles were reversed

An inch of wet plastic: the channel's traversed

It could be you sailing to England from France

Did the world steal your soul, please just give hope a chance?

SINKING

I did not wave at you my dear, I was just
simply drowning

The clear horizon, sky so blue, my freckled
brow was frowning

But you were buying ice-cream and you did
not see me wave

Too late for you to see me sink, no chance I
could be saved

Discarded like unwanted thoughts of some
forgotten place

How fast your memory faded as you soon
forgot my face

My frantic arm that reached out to the surface
of the sea

Was futile for you did not see, you did not
care for me

And later on, the tide came in, the crowd caused a commotion

But you strolled by and missed the din, devoid of all emotion

Locked up inside that head of yours, oblivious and mindless

As I washed up upon the shore of hope and human kindness

"How sad, how sad" the paper said, such tragedy and sorrow

A young life lost, a broken thread, chip paper for tomorrow

As seagulls circled, swooping low, the sun sank in the sky

My dear, I simply had to go, with no time for goodbye.

One day you could be in the sea and your arm might be waving

If Karma comes to call on you, how have you been behaving?

Could you count on those friends of yours to come and save the day?

Or will they be like most of us and look the other way?

A human life can be so small, a hand slips through a hand

Perhaps you shouldn't swim at all, stay safely on the land

When time and tide are turned on you, before you know you're sinking

You could end up as fortune's fool in a second worth of blinking

The savage foam may choke your words and seagulls mask your cry

Your tiny voice will not be heard and you may not know why

The loneliness that swallows you like some voracious shark

Will come and drag you down into the oceans deep and dark

A billion people stroll on by with eyes fixed on the sun

And yet you sense another's pain, are you the only one?

TWO FRIENDS

Sitting at the sea's edge watching the setting sun

Looking back on happy days when we were very young

Summers spent in sunshine, toes dipped in the sea

Golden days that sparkled bright, our friendship meant to be

Beach chairs close and cosy, fish and chips for tea

Hand in hand we sat there, so happy you and me

Walking to the pier's edge, ice-cream shared together

Knowing we had found a friend to warm our lives forever

Waiting in my deck chair, looking out to sea

Now there's only one seat, I know you wait
for me.

JUST A DAY

Don't ask me if my day was good or try to make it more

Than just a bunch of clustered hours in groups of twenty-four

I won't be drawn to give my thoughts on what life ought to be

And I won't have my heart exposed for anyone to see

No deep held wisdom to discuss for life is what it is

Just lip-service in borrowed time on mouths that never kiss

Existence : breathing in and out and sometimes missing breaths

So please don't make a fuss of me and don't you cause me stress

My silence is not emptiness, just simply, I won't add

Indulgent words to smooth the way or mask when I feel sad

I give to you the truth I hold and hope you will survive

When life we have is nothing more than us being alive

So I will ask you once again to leave and let me be

There's so much more to all of this than you will ever see

I will not offer platitudes as others try to do

I plant the seed of common-sense: the rest is up to you.

A SECRET …

And I have had the best of you, the best a life
can bring

The truest love to touch a heart and make a
spirit sing

You made a difference to a soul who had
before been broken

The secret saved and lesson learned, but shall
remain unspoken

So I have stolen something small, a gift from
you I've taken

A life that makes it all worthwhile, but my
soul was forsaken

The clue I'll give is in the eyes, the heart, the
smile and fingertip

The kindest heart to grace the world, the
softest hand and sweetest lip

Your legacy remains my gift no matter how life harms you

The signs of you will still endure when life no longer warms you

For I have got the best of you, a love that's like no other

So I am glad to see you laugh and share life with another

But one day when your bones are old, I might just share my secret

I stole the very best of you, and sold my soul to keep it

Each day brings me a sense of you, those sweet eyes and that soft voice

The humour and the wisdom knowing I have made the best choice

For love like that could never end I'll carry it forever

The greatest gift, you'll never know, we had a child together.

SMART LIFE

Love many people, but trust just a few

It's best if you paddle your own damn canoe

Sing when you're happy and cry when you're not

Be thankful for every small thing that you've got

Smile when you're lucky and chill when you're sad

Remember to balance the good with the bad

Don't harbour resentment, just shrug and move on

Look after your body, admit when you're wrong

Kiss lots of people and never be shy

Don't get yourself broken and don't make us cry

Waste not one second, this life can be short

Remind yourself happiness cannot be bought

Create a small difference in each person's life

(Success is not measured by absence of strife)

Make every day count, but no person too much

Put all your best effort in each thing you touch

Learn to be gentle and be a great friend

Keep a bag packed for that special weekend

Enjoy every moment and make it good fun

We only get "so many" turns round the sun.

DEAR TEACHER

That warm, caring voice bringing calm, sense and reason

Your patience abides, any time, any season

A rare special gift of just giving your best

You always dig deep when you're put to the test

Generations of children have passed through your care

You make schooldays better with kindness to spare

These words come to thank you for all that you do

The world needs more bright, thoughtful people like you

So thank you dear teacher for helping us shine

You're saving humanity, one child at a time

ON THE SPECTRUM

I'm just one small person who's different to you

I don't see the world in the same way you do

I feel like I'm lost here, unsafe in my class

This world that we live in keeps spinning too fast

Too much information comes flooding my way

It's so hard to cope with it day after day

Bright lights and loud noises all hurt me too much

My senses bombard me - I don't cope with touch

I'm not being awkward, just doing my best

I'm juggling emotions that fill up my chest

If only you'd see just how *hard* I have tried

And how much the worries can build up inside

You all see a classroom, I just see my chair

I don't always 'get' things and nothing is fair

If only you'd see things from my point of view

Perhaps then you'd like me the way I like you

We're on the same planet, our lives, parallel

Your life looks so perfect, I'm trapped in a shell

So please do not judge me, I am doing my best

My heart's crying out to be "just like the rest"

Things could be so different, you're lucky you see

I could have had your life and you could be me.

ELLIS ISLAND

When I am gone and turned to dust, I'd like to end up here

All sprinkled in the Hudson, cast me on the wind, my dear

The feet of lady liberty bear testament and truth

Engraved in stone, with heartfelt care, are words that fired my youth

My heart was filled with passion at the message I did read

A faithful poem carved in stone that stayed with me, indeed

Transcending every generation : promises were sworn

That any feet which tread this path will find the welcome warm

There was a sense of hope for me that words could not convey

That pierced my soul and stayed with me on that cold winter's day

The air was lit with shimmering light, the sky was golden brown

I travelled half the world to see the sun as she lay down

The ferry took me to a place my father's feet had stood

As space in time so far away, but deeply in my blood

And Ellis Island bears his name to mark that he was here

I pause in winter sunshine as I wipe away a tear

From foreign shores to Yankee soil and wrapped in love and pride

I follow in his footsteps as I search the world outside

An immigrant, a cheeky lad, in nineteen twenty-two

At seventeen he left the farm and everything he knew

So I repeat his journey as I stand beneath this lamp

Forgive me for a moment as my cheek is feeling damp

His spirit of adventure somehow found a home in me

One day my child will understand a man
needs to be free

You'll read those words beneath the lady
guarding this new shore....

New York, New York will call you back, full
circle, here once more.

●●●

WELL-LIVED

A life lived so fully, has reached earthly end

But lives in the memory of each trusted friend

A special place saved in the corners of hearts

Sustaining through sad times now we are
apart

From bride at the altar who shared his new
smile

To children who held loving hands for a
while

The memories and moments are wrapped safe
and warm

Secured by soft ribbons, packed safely from
harm

Such love can't be counted, and time can't destroy

The happiness filling our lives up with joy

The wisdom and knowledge in stories he'd tell

The legacy that lives in the ones he loved well

His brave light will help us to flourish for years

A life well-lived, filled up with sunshine and tears.

■■

MILLIONAIRE

There is an island far away, beside the deep blue sea

Where waits a man with happy eyes, his soul has been set free

He does not feel the pain of life, he wears a peaceful smile

He knows that he was loved on earth, now he can rest awhile

He paid his dues a thousand times for he was truly brave

And we can't thank him now for all the people he has saved

The wise man knew that freedom comes from never selling out

And a giant pile of things to love is not what life's about

True passion for experience replenishes the soul

Just being rich in stocks and shares should never be your goal

True wealth cannot be measured by the assets that you crave

A bank account is fine, but it won't buy a bigger grave

The man, he was a millionaire of all that he surveyed

His fortune not dependent on the money he was paid

A lifetime of adventures was stored up inside his mind

And that made him the richest man that you will ever find.

. . . .

WEDDING QUEEN

Today is such a special day and dreams have all come true

For all the love that's in this room begins and ends with you

You are so dear to everyone and have been all these years

So today we only want to see you crying happy tears

This will be the finest wedding we have ever seen

So we will raise a glass to you, our lovely wedding Queen.

••

JUST GAMING

Sit with me in the shadows and play just a little more

Let's have another try my friend, to beat our finest score

The time will fly so very fast when I sit here with you

We're peaceful for our Mums at last, and winning's what we do

Soon we both will be grown up with children of our own

Remembering all the fun we had before games were outgrown.

....

A SHIP CALLED HOPE

A boy set sail in a ship called Hope, with the stars set to guide his heart

On his journey to find an unknown land where his life had a brand new start

For his world was a cruel and empty space where it seemed time would just stand still

And the lure of the sea was calling him as she promised him an extra thrill

But the salty air would brush his cheek and the sunlight would take its toll

While the curve of the earth would disappear as the sunset caressed his soul.

■■■

BI-POLAR BEAR

It's easy to be broken by this brutal world
we're in

Some days just feel unbearable, it's so hard to
begin

Today I can't face anything, the stairs feel
like a mountain

My tears are wretched: pouring like a painful,
endless fountain

The sunshine feels too bright today, it burned
my eyes again

I close the curtains knowing that today is not
my friend

I don't think I will make it out, my heart is
wrapped in fear,

I cannot hold my head up and I don't want people near

My bones feel heavy lately, something in the air it seems

My sleep is broken and I'm being haunted by my dreams

Can't pull myself together, all this sadness weighs me down

And yet I'm so exhausted I can hardly raise a frown

I should wrap myself in kindness: pour some coffee, read a book

And when I'm brave I'll raise the blind and take a second look …

HATERS

Victory does not crown the just, it tears their souls apart

But fight and hurt they surely must, and break each other's heart

The dreadful choice to kill a man, who any other day

Might happily share a cup of tea to while the hours away

What guides a man to vilify and cause the blackest tears

Embracing hatred all the while and wasting precious years

And who decides our enemy and tells us who to hate?

Encouraging us to disrespect our weak and feckless mate

A power bigger than we are sells us this bitter dream

To make us hate each other, they are meaner than they seem

A clever stunt to fool us while their deeds are done in shade

Distracting us from what is done when rules are being made

Obedient and faithful to the narrative we read

Just blinded by the smoke and mirrors, we are fooled indeed

A dead man walking in his shoes and barely breaking stride

Somnambulant, as hell awaits him, full of broken pride

So smug's the colour that he wears to keep
him safe and warm

And hatred fills those bloody veins while
wishing others harm

Misguided and so out of touch with all
humanity

A cushioned world that keeps him safe from
all reality

But he is not your enemy, who walks that
beaten track

Look higher up to see your foe and always
watch your back.

The bitter pill is swallowed up like manna
from the gods

There's every probability you'll never beat
the odds.

THE PATRIOT

I know you wear your poppy proudly there on
your lapel

But you just walk right past me on the steps
of your hotel

And when I'm in the doorway of that local
shop near you

You spare your change to help me, but I'll bet
you never knew

The last steps that I ever took on feet that
were my own

Were taken far away from here, while you
were safe at home

My face is badly scarred, those stitches don't
belong to me

I know you spot the damage, but there's more
you never see

I'm living here in darkness, I will never see
again

The fear and terror lives in me, my mind feels
searing pain

My soul was cut to pieces, the best part of me
is torn

My comrades fell around me and their
friendship's what I mourn

Their courage bought your freedom, but they
were not bitter men

If the question came to call us up, we'd do it
all again

Inside we are all heroes although that's not
what you see

We sleep on floors and doorways so that you
can all be free.

.

FLOWER GARDEN

In this garden filled with flowers there must
be some leaves that fall

Peaceful memories fill the hours, tears are
shed despite it all

Life's a journey to be cherished, time's a gift
we can't all share

Memories in our minds embellished, deep our
pain the more we care

While the fates have shown no mercy, eternal
love is never ended

As you follow on this journey, dance as if
your life depended

And although his earthly presence will not
grace this world again

There's an overwhelming essence in the early morning rain

Feel the sunshine on your shoulder, see the sparkle on the sea

You know his eyes will not grow older, you'll see his heart has been set free

While the searing pain is glancing, never seeming to subside

Life is better when you're dancing, love will always be your guide

In the quiet of the evening when the stars are overhead,

Raise a glass instead of grieving, celebrate this life instead.

CHRISTMAS TIDINGS

Everyone's lonely on this little blue dot

Some people have everything while others do
not

No matter the colour of hair, eyes and skin

We all get so broken, so lonely within

The Christmas lights twinkle: the shops call
our name

They beckon us in spending plastic again

Out on the wet pavement the homeless man
sits

Reminding us life's still a battle of wits

How far have we come since the biblical days

Has man learned the secret of mending his
ways

Why can't we be kinder, make fairness our way

We're all still alone at the end of the day.

NEW YEAR'S TOAST

Long after bells and midnight chimes

And folks have shared their Auld Lang Synes

The corks from champagne bottles cracked

With tables cleared and chairs all stacked

Our time to sit while we reflect

On last year's resolutions wrecked

To ponder on mistakes we made

With conscience searched and fault replayed

We sit and mull on life's true path

A time to sit and share a laugh

For life is full of sliding doors

A foolish heart can soon be yours

And fate can be a fickle friend

To rob you of a happy end

Be kind then to your humble heart

And pledge to make a brand new start

An open heart will set you free

If absent friends are haunting thee

Toast loved ones who are far apart

Pay forward kindness with your heart

Stand tall and raise a glass to you

Another year, you made it through!

THE NARCISSIST...

A look inside those cold blue eyes

One glance will tell the tale

I'm not a consolation prize

My heart is not for sale

The ice that sits inside your soul

So frozen it won't melt

You scored inside an open goal

Your heartbeat can't be felt

An honest thought can not be yours

While you deceive yourself

And you are just a real lost cause

So tragic on your shelf

And yet you stay so bitter

Having all that you desired

It seems you lost your glitter

Despite all you have acquired

So I will look right through you

Knowing I did all I could

There's no one left to help you

The answer: you're no good.

THE SECRET OF SUCCESS IS
SINCERITY - IF YOU CAN FAKE THAT,
YOU'VE GOT IT MADE ~ GEORGE
BURNS

MY GENTLE MUM

Let me rest in quiet with you, kiss my cheek and hold my hand

Do not ask me to remember, or try to help me understand

I'm confused beyond believing, and I'm sick and sad and lost

But I really need you near me, care for me at any cost

Please don't lose your patience with me, don't give up on me, or cry

I can't help my strange behaviour, and can't reach you, though I try

Please remember I will need you when the rest of me is gone

I need you here to stand beside me, to love me 'til my time is done.

(THE ADHD POEM)

You all look like you are in SLO-MO

With mouths moving silent and blurred

My mind is just racing so swiftly

Whatever you say can't be heard

I'm tapping my foot while you're speaking

Just praying that you will speed up

I swear I can hear your shoes squeaking

And why is it you can't keep up?

A billion thoughts enter my headspace

A million nerves you're getting on

My brain thinks it's running a long race

My mind does not seem to belong

Ideas take up all my patience

I never know when to be quiet

I know I should just try to listen

But I don't have time left to try it

You're looking at me like I'm crazy

I'm looking at you just the same

You think I landed from a strange planet

A new one that hasn't a name

This ADHD is a blessing

It helps me see things in a flash

But it's such a pain when I'm thinking

When I'm in this mood I will crash

I'm sorry you don't understand me

I probably seem like I'm mad

It isn't a skill I requested

At times it can make me feel sad

So bear this in mind when you see me

Don't measure me like it's a test

I can't change myself for the better

Because I'm already my best !

A square peg could fit in a round hole

By knocking the sides off, it's true

The process is damaging my soul

Who said it was right to be you?

A CHILD WITH A SPECIAL NEED WILL
INSPIRE YOU TO BE A SPECIAL KIND
OF PERSON

TINY SNOWDROP

Crystal snowflakes softly fall and mingle with my tears

I can't recall when they began, it somehow feels like years

The silent snowdrop gently bends amid the crisp, cool air

She holds her head above the ground, aloft through my despair

I never get to see you grow and I can't hold your hand

The dreams I built inside my mind are castles in the sand

The hopes I had are melted and yet the ice still fills my heart

I carry you inside me so we'll never be apart.

SCARLETT

I know you're out there somewhere and I
guess you're far away

But I never got to tell you all the words I had
to say

This life can be a challenge some days barely
seem to start

It's hard to make a jigsaw from the pieces of
your heart

I look for signs around me and I try my very
best

I'm always finding feathers and I spot the
robin's breast

You have not been here lately, haven't seen
you for a while

I try to make the best of things and fake my
famous smile

Some days I get so angry, get so cross about the world

A wicked one that separates a mother from a girl

Tonight I'll try to find you in the stars that light the sky

I did not ask for too much, just a chance to say goodbye.

MY BOY

The universe could never steal the sunshine
from your smile

So I'll sit here and think of you, and hold you
for a while

Remembering how we used to laugh at funny
things you'd do

Such comfort as the day stands still each time
I think of you

For me the world has not moved on from
when we said goodbye

So hard to come to terms with this no matter
how I try

Despite how busy life becomes, wherever I
may go

My love for you can never fade, I'm certain
that you know

I miss you more than words can say and long to hear your voice

But fate has not been kind to us, we never had the choice

This world was never meant for you and your heart's been set free

So I'll carry you inside my heart, most precious part of me.

REBECCA

A tiny rose grew softly, warm and fragrant in
the sun

Her petals rich as velvet, stretching out to
everyone

So pretty that she shaded all the other blooms
somehow

The brightest pink and sweetest bud that
heaven would allow

A tiny bluebird came to call and ask the rose
her name

But she was dancing on the air, her heart he
could not claim

Then later she was still and so he joined her
and he stayed

Delighted to have found a friend to share his serenade

The hours passed so quickly as he sang his summer song

She sat beneath the tree with him, the sunshine was so strong

She turned her head a little reaching out into the light

The sun was far too wicked and his beam was burning bright

Her poor parched petals faltered leaving tender heart displayed

And so she leaned away to try and shelter in the shade

The darker foliage hid the rose to keep her safe from view

The tiny flower faded and did not know what to do

Then heaven's hand reached out to pluck the petals one by one

The garden lost it's glory when the precious rose was gone

So sadly that the sweetest rose was taken from our view

But she is not forgotten every time that spring is new.

"I WOULD SAVE YOUR LIFE EIGHT TIMES A DAY IF ONLY I COULD"
Snorkmaiden - Comet in Moominland ~ Tove Jansson

TO INFINITY AND BEYOND

When life no longer warms my bones and I
am turned to dust

Remember all the days we shared, our bond
of love and trust

And if the harshest winter winds blow in your
lovely face

Stand tall and face the fear you feel and live
your life with grace

For time can never steal from us the true love
that we share

Just look around for signs of me and you will
find me there

A feather dropped upon your path, a robin's
scarlet breast

My spirit comes to comfort you at every painful test

I will not falter at your side, my heart will shelter you

So even on the darkest days I'll always pull you through

Remember that our souls are linked by our unspoken bond

I carry your heart in my heart, to infinity and beyond.

BABY

He gripped my little finger, then his baby
hand unfurled

And I learned how a tiny tot can change
somebody's world

I would have paid attention had I known he'd
grow so fast

Those special times are treasured, locked
away inside the past

As life moves on, he makes me proud, that
cannot be denied

No longer cool to show it so I lock my love
inside

One day the world will move him on and
we'll be far apart

And though he has outgrown my lap, he can't
outgrow my heart.

"I WOULD LIKE TO LIVE IN A WORLD WHERE A CHICKEN CAN CROSS THE ROAD WITHOUT HAVING HIS MOTIVES QUESTIONED" ANON

STONE HEART

A solid stone sits in my heart, your loss
cannot be measured

Such space you left now we're apart, the
memories of you, treasured

Each day we live without your smile, as
empty as a chasm

We try to make the best of it, with lost
enthusiasm

The sun was brighter with you here, the days
were longer too

Instead the stars are brighter now (the biggest
one is you)

I'd sell the shoes I'm standing in to have you
here with me

To have you back just one more day, but you have been set free

The earthly worries that we shared aren't sitting on your shoulder

You stay as lovely as you are, your smile does not grow older

But we cannot replace your voice, the joy you brought each day

The ringing of your laughter and the funny things you'd say

So we must be content to sit with our memento box

We hug it to our wasted hearts and think about you lots

Our feelings stay closed down for now, confusion makes us numb

Awakening with our eyes tight shut, afraid when day's begun

We fool ourselves that we were wrong and you've not gone to stay

If we could just pretend again and keep *that* day away

Perhaps we could feel better if we thought we had a choice

A billion people fill my world, but I still miss your voice

My wishful thinking will not help, this time it's really true

A lovely person as you were, this world was not for you

The questions race around my mind, I'm too afraid to ask

So I must shake myself awake, it's such a daunting task.

STOLEN STAR

I stole a star out of the sky and held it close to me

I borrowed it for just a while where only I could see

The sparkle and the brilliance that brought a wealth of joy

A fluffy haired, adorable and precious little boy

I watch him grow and cherish him, a golden ray of sun

He makes his way out in the world and my work's nearly done

It's hard to reconcile that he could ever be this tall

I look at him with half a glance, he's back to being small

My day comes to a standstill as I travel back
in time

Returning to the moment when I first knew he
was mine

He gripped my little finger as his baby hand
unfurled

Amazing how a tiny soul can change
somebody's world

I would have paid attention had I known he'd
grow so fast

I blink and then I'm back again, from
memories of the past

As life moves on he makes me proud, that
cannot be denied

But it's not fair to show it so I lock my love
inside

One day the world will move him on and we'll be far apart

Although he has outgrown my lap, he won't outgrow my heart.

IF YOU ARE COMPLETELY EXHAUSTED AND DO NOT KNOW HOW YOU ARE GOING TO GIVE SO MUCH OF YOURSELF, DAY AFTER DAY – YOU ARE PROBABLY AN AMAZING PARENT

JUST 'TECHNO' NOTICE

What's happened to our lifestyle? It seems a bit "messed-up"

We're closer to our FB friends and real friends don't hook up

The children are all texting and they have no time to look

They're missing out on wonder and no-one reads a book

It looks like we've forgotten how we're all supposed to live

We're isolated units, and we're using apps to give

We miss those human moments, and how they kept us close

Alone inside our inbox, we are sad and we're morose

So how can we reverse this trend, remember who we were

Before we gave up trying and we still knew how to care

The lonely and the fragile seem so useless to us now

Our 'selfies' are what matter, but we've lost ourselves somehow

So next time you are outside raise your chin and take a look

The planet still has beauty and the world's an open book

Do it while we still have tigers, and monkeys swing in trees

Remember that you're lucky, because all of this is free.

All Gave some, some gave all …

THE ACCRINGTON PALS

Seven hundred men from a sleepy town,
seven hundred friendships bonded

As the call went out to the nation's men,
seven hundred hearts responded

Lord Kitchener's troops were called to arms
as the solemn hour was striking

Each platoon comprising fearless pals met the
call as fast as lightning

The Great War called their spirits on, leaving
mills unmanned and silent

Seven hundred men bade brave farewells,
there was no time to be frightened

Their hearts too young to comprehend all the
dangers set before them

Seven hundred tear-soaked mothers' cheeks did their best to keep decorum

For those northern lads with their golden hearts, ever true and unpretentious

Cheerful banter kept their spirits buoyed to light up the darkest trenches

Patriotic souls were steeled to the core and their courage brightly shone

As remembrance of their homes grew feint, and yet still they soldiered on

Their gift of freedom shall endure and their memory shall be treasured

For we owe those brave young men our lives, never quantified nor measured

They're forever in our humble prayers for the price they paid was boundless

Such brave young men who gave their all,
and the debt we owe countless

…Seven hundred left that sleepy town, but
only seven men returned

A generation taken in its prime, such a bitter
lesson learned

Those Accrington pals stood side by side,
each man joined up at the shoulder

Fearless comrades who will never fade, for
their souls shall not grow older.

BROKEN BRITAIN

Alone in the dark as the winter winds blow

Stands one lonely wheelchair, parked up in the snow

Some turn a blind eye for they simply don't care

How shameful and sad that this world's so unfair

No shelter for you when you're out on your own

Life drags you right down when the pavement's your home

The people keep passing, too busy to stop

Just looking away as they race to the shop

Wealth is not a passport to heaven, they say

While putting their gloves on and walking away.

A WELL-KEPT SECRET

There's a special parents' secret some of us
will share

Hearts are laden down with grief too
cumbersome to bear

And many try to give us comfort with a
thoughtful word

But though they act with good intention, kind
words go unheard

For once a child is taken from you, the world
has been destroyed

Days pass quickly, cold and empty, nothing
fills the void

We're a special bunch of people, broken tears
to spare

Robbed of hope and happiness, just shells of
who we were

If the world was based on justice, parents
would not suffer so

How can it be right or fair to lose a child
before they grow?

If there's any consolation, it's from sadness
strength is taken

While the journey is such torture, hope exists,
we're not forsaken

And while there is no reason why this
sentence could be fair

Time will sometimes bring acceptance of the
cross we bear

Learn to recognise the others, who also wear
a broken smile

Spot the signs before they're mentioned, lend your shoulder for a while

Don't look back at what you're missing, never offer platitude

You know just how hard each day is, fill your heart with gratitude

So if you are one amongst us, exclusive membership's been earned

You don't need to wear the T-shirt, just pay forward what you learned

Make a point of being kinder, use your loss to build a bridge

We cannot bring back our loved ones, stolen time can't be relived

One thing's certain life's unfair, that's simply just the way it is

But memories held cannot be stolen, neither can your loved one's kiss

MY NANA'S COAT

My Nana's coat is on the hook, the same place it was left

My Nana is not here today, and I feel so bereft

She is not here to smile at me or make the day seem better

I'll never see her script again upon a card or letter

I did not get to say goodbye because I was too busy

But now she's gone to heaven and the thought makes me feel dizzy

I wonder : did she realise, and did she ever know?

That out of all my relatives, I truly loved her so

She had those twinkly eyes of hers that told me all along

That she was always on my side, no matter what went wrong

So I will hug her empty coat, left hanging by the stair

And think about my lovely Nan and why life's so unfair.

RETAIL THERAPY

Your eyes are making promises I simply can't ignore

That silent, yet appealing pull that I have felt before

You have the kind of dashing smile that opens every door

We both know you're a bad boy and of that we can be sure

You never let it hold you back, you leave us wanting more

And I'm not one to hesitate, impulsive to the core

When passion takes control of me and all my senses roar

One nanosecond later, a belt buckle hits the floor

A meeting of two hearts and minds, but we both know the score

Just pull yourself together girl, you're shopping in a store

It seems that I had drifted off to yesterday once more

I shake off all those memories and the tears begin to pour

I start to browse the section of this famous superstore

Where I can hide my feelings best and keep this heat obscure

For you are with your wife and children: family you adore

My memory has just "played me" so I head out to the door.

DEAR MR MOONPIG

Dear Mr Moonpig (the man who makes the cards)

I need to ask assistance for a task I'm finding hard

I'm writing you from heaven, which I'm sure you'll think is odd

But they haven't got a card shop so I need a word with God

My mission is quite easy, I just need to find a card

To send to my poor mummy, she finds Christmas really hard

I looked at all the websites trying carefully to choose

There's every kind of card out there, but none
that I can use

So that is why I'm writing, can't you see what
you can do?

The other mums all get a card, she's still a
mummy too

She writes for other people, typing late into
the night

I know she's keeping busy so her tears are out
of sight

She mentions me quite often but she's stuck
down there on earth

I wanted to say thank you and remind her
what she's worth

So thank you Mr Moonpig, I just know you'll
try your best

I gave you my idea now can you please do the rest…

… a month has passed already and it's nearly New Year's Eve

I tried to send a Christmas card, but nothing's been received

I guess you did not get the brief, I left it far too late

I couldn't send her *anything* to let her know she's great

Please put this in your diary and just promise me you'll try

I know she's feeling empty 'cos we NEVER said goodbye.

SUCH A SADDO

Just grab a tiny violin from the violin
dispenser

It does not take a genius or folk signed up
with Mensa

To see we have a problem here, your ego took
a hit

The centre of the world just moved, and
you're no longer it

Now you have been replaced I guess that
must be pretty hard

To realise that you no longer hold the
winning card

He's younger than you used to be, he's
younger than you now

And I have had an upgrade.. you have been replaced somehow

The thoughts of you had worn me down and sent me round the bend

The Gods were looking kindly and they sent me a new friend

Ironic consolation prize for sitting on my ass

I'm sorry mate the gig is up, and you have been outclassed

For I have hit the jackpot and it seems you lost your crown

Revenge for all the times you tried your best to keep me down

Pyjama life was lonely sitting there waiting for you

Stuck in the bedroom drinking wine and making myself blue

Depression was my hobby then, it helped my thighs stay thin

How sad I was to wait for you just sipping on the gin

Your name was etched upon my heart, I tried to tear it out

With fingernails, and vodka shots, and buckets of self-doubt

You knew I would have died for you, and sold my very soul

For you saw love as weakness and scored in an 'open goal'

But you were 'cheap as chips' my dear, but hey, what can you do?

My guardian angel needs a raise, she got me over you

So sit there as the roles reverse and karma does her thing...

And I'll sit here and watch the sunlight catch my diamond ring!

THE ROOM

I'll take you through a tiny door that only
sadness knows

We'll wander where the mums and dads are
counting baby toes

Up in the room that's filled with light, and
hearts upon the wall

All left by tiny angels, for their wings were
far too small

Those hearts are really special, they're all
made of tiny feet

They represent the baby ones whose hearts no
longer beat

These parents feel the pain each day, the
silence morning brings

When life has taken everything, exchanged
for angel wings

They're broken, yet they try their best, brave smiles are all around

Alone and yet there seems to be a piece of common ground

A unity that joins their lives linked up like daisy chain

A comfort in each others eyes to face a world of pain.

MORE AUSTERITY

I sit here on the sofa, sipping slowly on the gin

I think about the TV news, and what a mess we're in

I ought to get some shopping in, the cupboard's looking bare

I tried to order it on-line, but there's simply nothing there

There are no slots again this week, I'll have to go myself

Another wasted journey when there's nothing on the shelf

I'm dodging in and out the aisles, like that 'old guy' on strictly

No peaceful stroll around the store, I'm grabbing things quite quickly

I'm mindful of the price increase caused by "the war in Russia"

And we're all living on a prayer ~ whatever we can muster

Dear Jamie you have no idea, such pressure that I'm under

There's no asparagus today, just jars of peanut butter

Perhaps I'll rustle up some soup with stock cubes and some pasta

That's not the kind or cordon bleu that I was really after

I guess there's always beans on toast, my 'friend' from days at uni'

But there's no beans again today, the future's looking gloomy

I feel like giving up the fight, or foraging the hedgerow

I feed the kids on crackers, it's no wonder they don't grow!

I AM SO GREEDY

I like to see my teeth marks in the butter on
my toast

I love the glaze of goose fat on potatoes as
they roast

I never stint on calories, they simply take a
seat

I am a walking advert for the naughty things I
eat

I love the smell of fresh baked bread that
wafts up in the air

I should not be so greedy, but I'm sorry, I
don't care

I love to see the bubbling of a soup I made
from scratch

Devouring the ingredients as recipes are hatched

Just let me loose on fluffy cake and fine patisserie

Or Cornish cream tea loveliness is how to get round me

Pavlovas are adorable and crème fraîche is sublime

Oooh, freshly grated parmesan will get me every time

The Friday queue outside the chippy *always* pulls me in

And I love snacks and peanuts when I'm sipping on my gin

I relish purple wrapping on that favourite bar of choc

(It seems it's always tea time when I'm looking at the clock)

Mr Hollywood from Bake-Off how I love to have you near

Seduce me sweet Nigella, draw me in oh Jamie dear

I am capable of eating every single thing I see

I'll never be your skinny friend, of that I guarantee.

DEAR BULLY

You hate yourself and that is why

You break my heart to make me cry

You bully me because you hurt

While rolling me in mud and dirt

Just break the mould and try your best

Don't be a loser like the rest

You have a heart, just use it then

Just think that through and change, my friend.

THE LOAN

He said: I have a little child to lend you for a while

A tiny star to warm your world and reignite your smile

With innocence and tenderness to make your heart feel whole

The love you searched for all your life, to mend your broken soul

But don't forget this is A LOAN, he said with a wry glance

Don't build those hopes up or believe this is your lucky chance

And with those words still in the air he disappeared from sight

The magic glow the baby brought just vanished in the night

The morning came and things grew cold, the miracle had ended

Her empty arms hung at her side, her heart could not be mended

She cried herself to sleep and then she cried herself awake

And pondered if she was to blame for making a mistake

At once a dark and heavy cloak fell all around her shoulder

The light grew dim and time stood still, except her face grew older.

YOU ARE <u>NOT</u> DEAD

Such fools they are, you are NOT dead !!! ~
your voice still rings inside my head

The wisdom of the tales you told still
resonates, and won't grow old

Your laughter lives inside of me.You are
NOT dead !!!You've been set free

From obligations you fulfilled. Your spirit
lives, you are not killed!!!

Reminders of you fill the air ~ You're all
around me - everywhere

Such pain of loss unquantified ~ I won't
accept that you have died

You kept yourself in such good shape ~ I always thought you might escape

You have not gone, I know they lied. With crocodile tears that they all cried

And I just know you got away and lived to fight another day

We'll laugh about the tears they shed…Such fools they are, you are NOT dead!!!

L8 4 MOF*

Remember when I left you stood

Out in that dodgy neighbourhood

Thought you would be angry, I was wrong

Do you recall that feeble line

I used when I was not on time?

I thought that you might dump me, I was wrong

So long you waited on your own

And nearly robbed of watch and phone

I thought you'd blow a gasket, I was wrong

That time my hair would not 'go right'

We nearly had the biggest fight

And yet you stayed and waited, I was wrong

No words of anger or despair

You smiled and said you didn't care

I thought you'd lose your patience, I was wrong

So many times I made you wait

While I was in chaotic state

I feared that you'd grow tired, I was wrong

I never thought that I would know

How it would hurt to miss you so

I thought you'd live forever, I was wrong.

*(I'd be late for my own funeral)

209

SEPTEMBER SONG

September is just glorious, crisp mornings
start the day

The roses bloom, victorious, to have their
final say

The children buzz and chatter in school shoes
so fresh and new

Next week they will be scuffed again, but just
what can you do?

That 'pencil' smell that fills the air in every
hopeful class

With only thirty days it's sad September does
not last

The question we all ask ourselves is "should I bring my coat"

Then p.m. has the answer as the sun returns to gloat

But most of all I'm glad to say there's simply *so much* CAKE

The wedding and the birthday kind, a lot to celebrate

The precious Christmas babies have their birthdays in September

They have an extra twinkle (flakes of magic from December)!

The leaves are sitting on the trees, no sweeping paths for me

The evening sky is still so clear, the stars can help me see

September simply has *so* much, the harvests gathered in

We share the fruits of summer 'til the Autumn chills begin

If I could choose a month to leave this earthly home of mine

I'd like to pick September, she is simply just divine.

IF PLAN 'A' DID NOT WORK, DON'T PANIC,THE ALPHABET HAS 25 MORE LETTERS

(UNLESS YOU ARE SWEDISH)

SWEDEN

Our feet may leave Sweden, our hearts never
do

With so many things that I still need to do

Returning is never the easiest choice

The tears and emotions well up in my voice

I understand all that makes my soul complete

The miles melt away with a tiny heartbeat

You gave me my father, and all that is good

A viking lives here in my heart and my blood

So I thank the heavens for bringing me home

The light in my soul means I'm never alone.

REMEMBER ME, MY FRIEND

When I am gone and all that's left

Are lines upon a page

I don't want you to be bereft

Or think of me in rage.

Remember all our better years

Those not consumed by writing

Please don't hold onto pain and tears

To think of all our fighting.

I hope I gave you what you'd need

And did not waste a minute

The book of life was long, indeed

Our story featured in it.

I know you thought I made a fuss

My heart upon my sleeve

I tried to change the world for us

And share things I believe.

I hope I left something of me

That made your day feel brighter

And lent some positivity

To make your burden lighter.

I know it was a mystery

To understand my mind

But we had so much history:

The best friend I could find.

Remember this when hope seems far

You were the best part of me.

Our friendship lit a thousand stars

So don't you dare forget me.

Don't leave this book upon the shelf

Please read the lines I brought you.

Be true of heart and love yourself

The way I always taught you.

Despite how life can seem absurd

You know I'm glad I found you.

May all the sunshine from my words

Just wrap itself around you.

TO BAH OR NOT TO BAH(that is the question)

To Bah Humbug or celebrate, that truly is the question!

This happy season brings some time for quiet, calm reflection.

The joy of Christmas can be hard when you aren't quite invested.

So many jobs we have to do, our patience being tested.

We force ourselves to all take part while it's so overwhelming.

Those cards we write are sealed with love and joy that we are sending.

The spirit of our Christmas past is in our hearts and faces.

Like sugared crumbs of warm mince pies,
each memory leaves its traces.

A glass of whiskey by the tree, remembering
friends departed.

A tear of sadness on our cheek, and back to
where we started.

With shining eyes, like little tots, so hopeful
and excited.

The friends and family gathered in and
neighbours all invited.

Anticipation building up, will Santa bring his
reindeer?

Have we remembered everything ?(that's our
abiding fear)

At least there's Bublé in the car and Del Boy
in his van !

We welcome all those visitors as 'politely' as we can.

If you find yourself at breaking point and wish you had a rifle…

Console yourself with peanuts as you dive in sherry trifle!

Its time to stick Mariah on and give your lungs a blast.

Remembering the joys and tears of every Christmas past.

Put on a Christmas movie and make Baileys your best friend.

And I guarantee that you will fall asleep before the end.

Enjoy each tiny second of this Christmas, if you will…

January soon reminds us that we have to pay the bill.

To Bah Humbug or not to Bah, the question is just timeless…

You may as well embrace it then, and make this one your finest!

'Those who don't look for magic will never find it" Roald Dahl

STRICTLY ADDICTED

An hour before STRICTLY and all thru' the land

Installed on their sofas with glasses in hand…

Are all kinds of humans just glued to a screen

Excited, elated, addicted, it seems.

A passion for dancing is gripping the nation

The Saturday night slot filled with anticipation.

This growing obsession with Tango and Latin

Folk dressed in a flurry of sequins and satin.

We're all into watching it week after week

The lycra's so tight it can make your eyes leak!

We practise the moves in our tea breaks at work

Attempting to foxtrot and trying to twerk.

We samba the school run and waltz into stores…

Avoiding the ironing and dull household chores

Embracing our own inner Anton du Beke.

We watch Fred & Ginger (some look more like Shrek)

Just drive ourselves crazy attempting to groove

And even our grandpa is 'busting a move'

The final comes fast as we're into December

Then we are all waiting 'til its next September.

FEELING SEE-THRU

I want to see her back again, that happy,
laughing girl

The one who thought so much of you, she
tried to change the world

Her veins are full of too much love that weigh
her down on earth

She wants to see what's up above, and maybe
try rebirth

The spirit that shines out of her is fading as
we speak

Forgotten who she's supposed to be and
feeling really weak

Her head hurts and her skin feels thin, her
bones are old and dry

She tries her best to hold it in, too tired to
question why

Someone should keep her children safe and tell them twice a day

That they have made her heart feel warm, but she's too cold to stay

They made the journey all worthwhile and balanced out the bad

They showed her how to smile again and make her heart feel glad

A see-thru version of our girl is floating in the sky

She's off to learn to play the harp, no time to say goodbye.

THE MASKED MAN

That mask you are wearing just intrigues me,
I must say

You have the kind of sexy look you don't see
everyday.

I want to steam your glasses up, invade your
personal space

I wonder what you hide beneath that mask
upon your face.

You fascinate the bones of me, the mystery is
intriguing

But damn its my turn in the queue, I really
should be leaving.

DAD

You never said "I told you so "

Though you had every right.

You stood by me through every mess

And helped me fight each fight.

I never knew just what you did

'Til I had children too.

So I have grown up late in life

My thanks are overdue.

That daily grind that breaks us down

Can be so hard to bear.

The worry and the deepest fears

We're too afraid to share.

You made it all look easy

Though I know those times were tough.

Fate dealt a hand to break our hearts

Those stormy seas were rough.

Remember that I'm grateful though

For every hand you lent.

Each disappointment that I caused

Was never with intent.

The things you taught were priceless

Even though your voice was gruff.

The kindest hearts come wrapped in steel

To try and make us tough.

So if I haven't thanked you

I will tell you it's all true.

Despite the times I let you down

I tried to be like you.

My gratitude is due to you

As I remain impressed.

I'm glad I got to be your child

Our gene pool is the best!

ADIEU AND GOODBYE

I thank you all for showing up to send me on
my way

You're wearing all your finest things, so
here's my chance to say

I thank you from my very heart that we have
shared some time

The laughs and tears that we enjoyed have
made it all sublime

I've 'wandered lonely as a cloud' and danced
upon some bars

I walked the road less travelled, pitched my
tent under the stars

I lived and loved, I've lost and won, I cleaned my teeth and flossed

I've gambled every cent I had. I've held good cards and lost

But through it all I had good friends who held me when I fell

You have been my champions and you helped me live so well

I know I drove you crazy and I got on every nerve

But had such love through all my life, much more than I deserve

Life is not the breaths we take, it's not the things we own

It's all the memories we have made and all the love we've grown

And in this world a billion souls could pass each other by

But I was blessed to know you and although it's now goodbye

I'm thankful for the time we had and all we got to do

I will look for you again my friend, the next time I pass through

And if I'm lucky one more time, we'll do it all again…

So get your glad rags ready, I'll be back for you my friend.

"It will be all right in the end, if it's not all right, it's not the end".

THE END.

"Let everything happen to you: Beauty and terror…Just keep going …No feeling is final"

Rainer Maria Rilke (Jo Jo Rabbit)

AFTERWORD:

Thank you to my dear friends for supporting my little hobby all these years. Thank you for all the lovely pens and notebooks and kind words you constantly furnish me with. You are my champions: RJJ, JP1&2,Karen,Tanya Doll,Charlotte,Karen,Mark,Claire,Tracey Jane, AMP66 & The Pearsons, EDY & Mr P, TP. Kathy W. Lloyd:quiet genius. Sally : Nasturtiums and Delphiniums. Brum Crew. Dear John and the Rouselings AWP. Polly - You know who you are x

ACKNOWLEDGMENTS:

Special thanks to Neil and Jonny for their constant inspiration and for providing the utterly fabulous cover picture : Never Stop Making Wishes, and for supporting my dream. We are truly kindred spirits.

Neil's inspirational artwork can be viewed throughout the Cotswolds and at : https://artistnelliehearn.co.uk/products/calendar-2023

Thank you to all my crazy and beautiful friends who encourage me, and also thank you to those *discourage* me. You all have valuable roles to play. Thank you to the Howcutts for being in my corner.

Thank you to my little brother for the reality checks. BEST OF (the)BEST.

Thank you to my parents for buying my first typewriter. Kaye, thank you for always helping me to keep my ducks in a row. Thank you to my amazing life-coaches: Paolo and Michael, for keeping me sane.

Finally a HUGE thank you to my dearest boys H and G, for tolerating some seriously half-hearted suppers while I was following my dream. You are my sunshine.

To everyone who chose to buy this book, I thank you!

"Never stop making wishes" xxx

Printed in Great Britain
by Amazon

11959697R00140